Life Lessons from the
Chapman Daily Adventures

Hello, God?

Chicaga A. Bauer

WestBow Press books may be ordered through booksellers or by contacting:

WestBow Press
A Division of Thomas Nelson & Zondervan
1663 Liberty Drive
Bloomington, IN 47403
www.westbowpress.com
1 (866) 928-1240

Because of the dynamic nature of the Internet, any web addresses or links contained in this book may have changed since publication and may no longer be valid. The views expressed in this work are solely those of the author and do not necessarily reflect the views of the publisher, and the publisher hereby disclaims any responsibility for them.

Any people depicted in stock imagery provided by Thinkstock are models, and such images are being used for illustrative purposes only.
Certain stock imagery © Thinkstock.

ISBN: 978-1-5127-7367-5 (sc)
ISBN: 978-1-5127-7368-2 (e)

Library of Congress Control Number: 2017901319

Print information available on the last page.

WestBow Press rev. date: 03/08/2017

WESTBOW
PRESS®
A DIVISION OF THOMAS NELSON
& ZONDERVAN

Dedication

In dedication to my Guiding Voice; to my most passionate inspirations: my two sons; to my parents, who have been a model of love; and to my best friend and love of my life, my husband... thank you for believing in me and supporting me on this journey.

Acknowledgments

First, I would like to thank My Heavenly Father for His Direction in this project. Thank you to my husband, sons, family, and friends for their encouragement and support. Thank you to my Illustrator, Ashley J. Wilson-Gaber, for her amazing illustrations and creative input. Thank you to my Writing Coach and Editor, MJ Schwader, for his patient guidance.

Preface

My purpose in writing this book is to encourage and equip children for a successful life journey. Each of my stories models a "Life Lesson" with an opportunity to teach our youth how wonderfully amazing they are and how each one of them are here on purpose for a purpose.

My hope is that all children who read my stories know that God created them and they are truly, perfectly loved. You see, that is where they will find their confidence of purpose, their ability to love, and their capacity to experience true joy and peace in their lives.

I am so grateful to have you with me on this journey to make a positive difference in the lives of the children around us. Together, we are lovingly impacting the world. After all, the children of today are the leaders of tomorrow.

May God bless you and keep you through each of the *Life Lessons from the Chapman Daily Adventures*.

Life Lesson #1: Hello, God?

What better way to embark on a journey than the only place it can start... the beginning! Genesis Chapters One and Two of the Bible teach us who we are and where we came from. God created the sky, the land and sea, the sun and the moon and the stars, and the day and the night. He created all the creatures from the tiniest to the most gigantic, and then He created us. Yes, we were created, not by accident, but absolutely on purpose. And do you know what? God created it all so that He could love us and have a relationship with us. Because of His Perfect Love we have the ability to love others.

"We love because He first loved us." – 1 John 4:19. God's unfailing love for us started it all. Are you excited to know that you are a part of His Plan?

You can make a difference by instilling in our youth what it truly means to be a "Child of God." I am so grateful that you are joining me on this journey, and that you are taking an active part in inspiring and encouraging our children.

Daniel is a smart, funny little boy who tends to have many questions, as most 5 year-olds do... especially at bedtime.

Mr. Chapman leaned in and gave Daniel one last tickle for the night.

"Time for bed, Big Guy," Mr. Chapman said as he kissed Daniel on his forehead.

"Buuuuuuttttt Daaaad," said Daniel in his bummed out voice.

Mrs. Chapman smiled and said, "Time to say your prayers."

Now Daniel has said his prayers for many, many nights.

In fact, he has been saying his prayers for so long that he can't remember not saying his prayers.

Questions started to rise up in his head. He couldn't help himself. He had to ask.

"Mom?" asked Daniel.

"Yes, Sweetie Boy," Mrs. Chapman answered.

Daniel liked it when she called him that... It made him feel special because it was her special name for him.

Daniel smiled and asked, "What exactly is a prayer... and exactly who is God? I know that I love Him, but who is He?"

"Those are great questions, Buddy," Mr. Chapman said as he knelt down next to Daniel's bed.

Mrs. Chapman smiled again and said, "A prayer is a conversation that you have with God."

"Yes, just like you talk and have conversations with Mom and me," added Mr. Chapman.

"You can talk to God about anything," said Mrs. Chapman.

"Everything good in the world is of God, and He loves you so very much. He made everyone special for a very important purpose."

Thoughts started to run through Daniel's head... He was thinking about what had happened earlier that day.

He had spilled his milk at school and made a mess all over the lunch table and onto the floor.

Mrs. Kowski, the school principal, hadn't looked too happy about it...

...and after school he wrestled too hard with his big sister, Grace, and got scolded by his mom.

"Does God love me even when I spill my milk at lunch and get scolded for wrestling with Grace?" Daniel asked.

Mr. and Mrs. Chapman chuckled.

Mrs. Chapman answered, "Yes, He absolutely does. His love for each one of us is more than we can even imagine."

"Can I tell Him that I'm sorry?" asked Daniel.

"Yes," replied Mr. Chapman.

"He already knows, but He wants us to tell Him everything...

...things that we are grateful for...

...things that we are sorry for...

...things that we dream about...

...things that we would like to do...

...Everything!"

"But... who is God?" asked Daniel.

"The Bible is the book that is all about God, written by God," said Mr. Chapman as he reached over and picked up Daniel's Bible from the bookshelf.

"God is who created everything. In the Bible, God teaches us how He made the earth, the day, and the night..."

...the land and the sea...

...and all the creatures on earth..."

"And people, too!" Daniel interrupted excitedly.

"Yes, and people, too," Mrs. Chapman agreed. She continued, "God is also love. He made us so that he could love us, and He wants us to have conversations with Him."

"I love God," Daniel said sleepily.

Now Mr. Chapman had a question for Daniel. "I know that you love God, Daniel... Why do you love God?"

"Because He made the earth and all of its stuff... and He loves me, even when I spill milk or get scolded...

...and He loved me first. He made me to love me," Daniel said most confidently.

"God is good," said Mrs. Chapman.

"Now let's say your prayers, Daniel," said Mrs. Chapman.

Daniel closed his eyes, folded his hands, and took a deep breath.

"I want this to be a good conversation," Daniel said thoughtfully. He began to pray.

"Hello, God? I know you're here and everywhere... God, thank you for everything that you have given to us... Thank you for loving me... Please bless my Mom, my Dad, my sister, Grace, and Guinea... my black lab, Bobo... my bulldog, Deacon, my Mimi, my Papa, my Grandpa, my Grandma... all my family, all my friends, all my teachers, and all my coaches...

Thank you, God... I love you... Amen."

Mr. and Mrs. Chapman smiled, then together said, "Aaaaa-men."

They gave Daniel a hug
and a kiss and said
goodnight.

"Goodnight," said Daniel, as he shut his eyes.

Daniel drifted off to sleep thinking about how much God loves him... and God loves you, too.

He made you very special.

May God bless you and keep you,
favor and protect you, Sweet One...

Sweet dreams.

About the Author

Chicaga A. Bauer holds a Bachelor of Science degree in Wellness and Health Promotion and an Associate degree in Liberal Arts with an emphasis in Communication. She loves to write and share her positive, inspirational stories and "Life Lessons." She lives in Pennsylvania and is happily married with two amazing sons.

About the Illustrator

Ashley J. Wilson-Gaber was inspired by art as a young child watching her favorite show, Sailor Moon. She attended the Art Institute of Pittsburgh as a graphic designer and illustrator. Ashley lives in Pennsylvania with her husband, two cats, and a chinchilla.

References

Life Application Study Bible: New International Version; Tyndale House Publishers and Zondervan Publishing House

The Everyday Life Bible: Containing the Amplified Old Testament and the Amplified New Testament; Faith Words Publishing

CPSIA information can be obtained
at www.ICGtesting.com
Printed in the USA
BVOW05s0608291017
498884BV00002B/9/P